DREAMS TAKE FLIGHT

DREAMS TAKE FLIGHT

The Girl Who Dared

Wing Commander

Ms. Ananya Sharma

Satish Puthran

SATISH PUTHRAN
DREAMS TAKE FLIGHT : The Girl Who Dared

DEDICATION

This novel is dedicated to the nation and to all the Indian armed forces aspirants, whether it's the Indian Army, Indian Navy, or Indian Air Force, especially women who have the courage and dare to fight against all the odds. They defy those who still believe they cannot achieve anything in their lives.

SATISH PUTHRAN
DREAMS TAKE FLIGHT : The Girl Who Dared

Table of Contents

ACKNOWLEDGMENTS

|| ॐ गणेशाय नमः ||

|| ॐ सरस्वती नमो नमः ||

|| श्री दुर्गापरमेश्वरी देवी नमः ||

This book wouldn't have been possible without the unwavering support of Lord Ganesha, Goddess Saraswati, and Sri Durgaparameshwari Devi from Kateel, Mangaluru, Karnataka, along with my parents especially my mom Mrs. Anita Puthran, my younger sister Ms. Sandhya Puthran, friends, relatives, well-wishers, all family members, and my India Authors Academy (IAA) mentor and book coach Mrs. Sweta Samota. Without all your support, this journey would have been impossible.

Stepping towards a new journey from ordinary to extraordinary, and then becoming an author.

Thank You.

INTRODUCTION

The Nepali language in this story is used solely to indicate its origin from a Nepalese village and is unrelated to any caste or religion.

E & O.E

NATIONAL ANTHEM

जन गण मन अधिनायक जय हे
भारत भाग्य विधाता

पंजाब सिन्धु गुजरात मराठा
द्राविड़ उत्कल बंग

विंध्य हिमाचल यमुना गंगा
उच्छल जलधि तरंग

तव शुभ नामे जागे,
तव शुभ आशिष मांगे

गाहे तव जय गाथा
जन गण मंगलदायक जय हे
भारत भाग्य विधाता

जय हे, जय हे, जय हे,
जय जय जय जय हे

TITLE IN DIFFERENT LANGUAGES

ಕನೊಕುಲು ಪಾರೊಡು

सपने उड़ान भरते हैं

সপোনবোৰে উৰণ লয়

ড্রিমস টেক ফ্লাইট

सपना उड़ान ले लेला

सपनां उड्डाण घेतात

ડ્રીમ્સ ટેક ફ્લાઈટ

ಡ್ರೀಮ್ಸ್ ಟೇಕ್ ಫ್ಲೈಟ್

सपना उड़ान भरते हैं

ഡ്രീംസ് ടേക്ക് ഫ്ലൈറ്റ്

स्वप्ने उड्डाण घेतात

सपनाहरू उडान भर्छन्

ਸੁਪਨੇ ਉਡਾਣ ਭਰਦੇ ਹਨ

स्वप्नाः उड्डयनं कुर्वन्ति

خواب اڏامندا آهن

கனவுகள் பறந்து செல்கின்றன

డ్రిమ్స్ టేక్ ఫ్లైట్

خوابوں کی پرواز

PREFACE

This is the story of a daring and highly ambitious girl, Ms. Ananya Sharma, who lives in a small abandoned village in Nepal.

It narrates her journey from dreaming to fulfilling her aspirations, as she confronts and overcomes all odds, ultimately paving her own path to becoming an officer in the Indian Air Force, in her own words.

DREAMS TAKE FLIGHT

In the quiet of night, where stars softly gleam,
Our dreams take flight on wings of a dream.
Through valleys of doubt and mountains of fear,
We soar ever higher, our vision sincere.

With each beat of hope, our hearts find their way,
Through the haze of tomorrow to the light of today.
For dreams are the whispers that guide us along,
They paint the horizon with hope's sweetest song.

So cherish each moment, each flicker of light,
For dreams take flight in the depths of the night.
With courage as wind, and passion our guide,
We journey together, side by side.

IN MEDIA RES

Ms. Ananya Sharma on becoming Indian Air Force Wing Commander to her parents in heaven

हेर्नुहोस अम्मा बाबा, म भारतीय वायुसेनाको
विंग कमाण्डर बनेकी छु, आज तपाईहरु सबै
मेरो साथमा हुनुहुन्थ्यो भने तपाईलाई
आफ्नो छोरीमा कति गर्व हुने थियो

See Amma Baba, i have become a Wing Commander of the Indian Air Force, if you all were with me today, how proud you would have been of your daughter.

उड़ान भर लो

उड़ान भर लो, सपनों की परवाज,

खुद पर भरोसा, नये अवसर आज

जीवन की धूल उठा कर, ऊँचाइयों की ओर,

मन में जो सपने हैं, पांव तले बिछाओ

डर को दूर भगाओ, हौसला बढ़ाओ,

हर कठिनाई से लड़ो, जीत का जश्न मनाओ

ज़िंदगी की चाह में, चलो आगे बढ़ो,

सपनों की परवाज को, आज हकीकत बनाओ

उठो, बढ़ो, पंख लगाओ,

सपनों की ऊँचाइयों को, आज छू जाओ

xvi

RETROSPECTIVE

SATISH PUTHRAN
DREAMS TAKE FLIGHT : The Girl Who Dared

Nepal is a beautiful country nestled in the Himalayas, known for its stunning landscapes, rich cultural heritage, and warm hospitality. It's famous for Mount Everest, the world's highest peak, and its diverse geography that ranges from lush plains to towering mountains. Kathmandu, the capital, is a vibrant city with ancient temples, bustling markets, and a blend of traditional and modern influences. Nepali culture is deeply rooted in Hinduism and Buddhism, reflected in its festivals, art, and architecture. The people of Nepal are known for their resilience and strong sense of community, making it a fascinating destination for travelers and adventurers alike.

In the shadow of Everest's lofty peak,
Where the Himalayas their majesty speak,
Lies a land of beauty, ancient and deep,
Where the soul of Nepal forever does seep.
From Kathmandu's bustling, vibrant heart,
To villages where traditions impart,
A tapestry woven with threads of old,
Stories of bravery and wisdom untold.
Temples rise with intricate grace,
Silent guardians of time and space,
Prayer flags flutter in the mountain breeze,
Carrying hopes skyward with ease.
In Nepal, where gods and mountains meet,

SATISH PUTHRAN
DREAMS TAKE FLIGHT : The Girl Who Dared

Where nature's wonders feel so sweet,
The spirit of resilience stands tall,
In every heart, in every call.
O Nepal, land of courage and grace,
Your spirit shines in every place,
Forever cherished, forever free,
In the hearts of those who yearn to see.

CHAPTER I

ख्वाबों की पंख

ख्वाबों की पंख लहराएं,

आसमान को छू लें हम

उड़ान भरे सपने हमारे,

हर मंज़िल पे जाएं हम

रात की चांदनी में लिपटे,

चलें आगे नयी राह पर

आओ मिलकर सपनों को पाएं,

हर पल बने खुशहाल हम

जीवन के रंग बहारें,

उम्मीदों का जलवा लें

हर इच्छा पूरी हो जाए,

ख्वाबों को बस हासिल करें

Born in the heart of Himalayas, a small abandoned village named Khangsar in Nepal having with strong tradition, superstition and poverty.

I am Ananya Sharma a small girl living with my mother, father and younger brother Aditya. In Nepali language i call my mother *'Amma'*, my father *'Baba'* and my younger brother *'Kancho Bhai'*.

My father name is Ram Kumar Sharma who is a very poor farmer, my mother name is Sarita Devi who is a government school teacher at Manang Quarter, Manang, Nepal while my younger brother Aditya studies in the same school where my mother teaches other children.

The villagers here believe in strong superstition. They always used to tell me that 'if any girl ventures outside her village, she may bring shame or dishonour to her family'. In the past my grandfather Baldev Singh, didn't allowed my mother to study coz of ongoing superstition in the village but my grandmother Saraswati Devi didn't believed in superstitions and she without making her daughter Sarita Devi venturing out of the village she allowed her to study and made her literate.

As my father was a very poor farmer he can't afford to teach both kids and hardly he can earn a penny for our living. My mother Sarita Devi took responsibility of teaching me & Aditya till Std 10th as i was keen in learning. She decided at that time itself will make her daughter's dream come true at any cost.

I was a smart and brilliant child since childhood and i often look up at the sky when Indian aircrafts flying above the sky and kept dreaming of joining 'Indian Air Force' and serve the nation. I used to listen to my mother teaching the school children this poem titled *'सपने की उड़ान'* and was mesmerized.

सपने की उड़ान

ख्वाबों की उड़ान ले जाए,
अंधेरों में भी रोशनी छाए

संदेहों के बादल हटाए,
मन की ऊर्जा स्वतंत्रता पाए

पंख फैलाए, अनजाने ऊँचाइयों तक,
संभावनाओं के खेतों में सीमित ना रहकर

हर इच्छा, एक प्रकाश चमका,
रात के ट्रायल्स के माध्यम से अग्रसर हुए

जो बवंडर भी आते हो और हवाएं चलती है,
सपने देखने वाले के दिल को हमेशा पता रहेगा

कि सपने की उड़ान है साहस की पंखों पर,
जहां भाग्य गाता है, वहाँ तारों के पीछे

तो सपने देखने के लिए हिम्मत रखो, पूरी ताकत से,
क्योंकि तुम्हारे सपनों में ही तुम्हें प्रकाश मिलेगा

तुम्हें ऊँचाईयों में उठाएगा, दृश्य से परे,

जहां सपने की उड़ान लेते हैं, असीम उड़ान में

The villagers always used to taunt me by saying this poem as it was very famous at that time.

गाउँकी केटी, सपनाका बारेमा,

हाम्रो मनमा उडान लिए, तर मान्छेहरू भन्छन् तिनी अनजान

"बेटी, तिम्रो लागि यी सपनाहरू महत्त्वपूर्ण छन्,

गाउँकी केटाहरूले मात्र घर-परिवारमा मात्र सोच्छन्"

उनको आँखामा प्रत्येक सपना चम्कदैछ,

तर मान्छेहरूको बोलीले मन धडक्छ

"तपाईंलाई इतिहासका सदियाँको परम्परा रहेको यहाँमा

पढ्नका कुनै फाइदा होला?"

पर उनले थामेनन्, हारेनन्,

सपनाहरूको उडानलाई मात्र थामेन्

अन्ततः एउटा दिन आयो, उनले ठुलो भएर देखायो,

गाउँकी केटीले, सपनाहरूलाई जित्न सक्यो

जनताले उनको उडानलाई हेर्दा, हेरान हुन्छन्,

गाउँकी केटीले सपनाहरूलाई पूरा गरेको देखिन्छ

✈ ✈ ✈

गाँव की छोरी, सपनों की दुनिया में,

मन में लिए उड़ान, पर लोग कहते हैं वह अनजान

"बेटा, तुम्हारे लिए ये सपने बड़े हैं,

गाँव की लड़कियाँ तो बस घर-बारे में ही सोचती हैं"

उसकी नज़रों में हर सपना चमकता है,

पर लोगों की बातों से दिल धड़कता है

"क्या फायदा इतने पढ़ने का,

जब गाँव की सदियों की रिवाज़ है यहाँ का?"

पर वह न रुके, न हारे,

सपनों की उड़ान को बस थामे

फिर एक दिन आया, वह बड़ी होकर दिखाया,

गाँव की छोरी, सपनों को जीता लाया

लोग देखे उसकी उड़ान को, हैरान हो गए,

गाँव की छोरी ने सपनों को पूरा किया पाया

CHAPTER II

सपना हर्दै उड्ने छ,

आँखामा चाँदीको ज्योति

पूरा गर्ने आशा र योजना,

पालन गरौं अनि ल्हासा

हाम्रो सपना उड्ने छ,

आकाशमा सँगै बादल

हामी सबै उड्नु पर्छ,

आफ्नो सपना पूरा गर्दै

Dreams always soar,
With the sparkle of silver in our eyes.
Hopes and plans to fulfill,
Let's nurture and cherish them.
Our dreams will fly,
Amongst the clouds in the sky.
We all must fly,
Completing our own dreams.

Although i was sad after listening to all the taunts given by villagers but i was not disheartened, i kept my passion of serving the nation brighten day by day fuelled by my admiration for Indian Air Force.

As my mother was government school teacher, after her school gets over i daily used to sit in library for hours, borrowing books and try to absorb every piece of information that i can lay my hands on regarding joining Indian Air Force. I often find myself daydreaming about a life beyond the village, a life where i can make a difference where i can give my younger brother Aditya and my parents a better life.

I not only being smart and brilliant but i was also interested in Mathematics and so i started to prepare myself for Indian Air Force entrance exams also alongwith reading other books.

The books which i used to read and refer were :

"The India-Pakistan Air War of 1965" by P.V.S. Jagan Mohan and Samir Chopra
- This book delves into the air operations during the 1965 war
between India and Pakistan, offering a detailed analysis of the IAF's role.

"The Mighty Eighth: A History of the Units, Men and Machines of the US 8th Air Force" by Roger A.

Freeman
- While not specifically about the Indian Air Force, provides a comprehensive look at the operations and experiences of an air force during wartime, offering comparative insights.

"Wings of Fire: An Autobiography" by Dr. A.P.J. Abdul Kalam
- Though primarily focused on Dr. Kalam's life and contributions to space and missile technology, it includes significant mentions of his involvement with the Indian Air Force and its influence on his career.

AFCAT (Air Force Common Admission Test) Guide by Ramesh Publishing House
- This book covers all sections of the AFCAT exam, including Verbal Ability, Numerical Ability, Reasoning, General Awareness, and Military Aptitude.

Quantitative Aptitude for Competitive Examinations by R.S. Aggarwal
- This is a good book for strengthening your quantitative aptitude skills, which are crucial for the AFCAT exam.

Objective General English by S.P. Bakshi
- For improving your English language skills, this book covers grammar, vocabulary, and comprehension.

General Knowledge 2023 by Manohar Pandey
- This book covers current affairs and general

knowledge topics required for competitive exams.

Let's Crack AFCAT - Air Force Common Admission Test by SSBCrack

- This is another popular guide that includes practice questions, solved papers, and tips for the AFCAT exam.

Wings of Fire: An Autobiography of Abdul Kalam (Hindi)/Agni Ki Udaan by A P J ABDUL (Wings of Fire का हिंदी अनुवाद Author APJ Abdul Kalam)

Previous Year AFCAT Topic-wise Solved Papers (2011 - 2023) with 5 Practice Sets for Flying Technical & Ground Duty Branches 9th Edition | Previous Year Questions PYQs | Air Force Common Admission Test

The Indian Air Force. Trends and Prospects – DTIC

CHAPTER III

ख्वाबों की उड़ान

ख्वाबों की उड़ान लेते हुए,

मैंने किया सफर शुरू,

जीवन के इन रास्तों में,

हर कठिनाई को चुनौती दी है

कांपती भीड़ में, ऊंचाईयों पर,

ख्वाबों का सफर जारी है,

उड़ान भर रहे हैं दिल के पंख,

हर असमान तक जाने की खातिर

इस दास्ताने में रात भर जागना है,

सितारों से बातें करनी है,

ख्वाबों के परवाने सब कुछ हैं,

उन्हें आकाश में उड़ान भरनी है

SATISH PUTHRAN
DREAMS TAKE FLIGHT : The Girl Who Dared

ज़िन्दगी की इस रवानी में,

हर कदम नया रंग भरेगा,

ख्वाबों की इस उड़ान में,

हर सपना सच होने को तरसेगा

I don't know from here onwards the path for which i choosed to become will go and its not so easy which i think it will be full of challenges and sacrifices.

To remain mentally and physically fit for Indian Air Force entrance exam i started now itself, daily morning and evening i ran 6 kms from Khangsar - Manang - Khangsar total 12 kms. It is really challenging to run on mountain trails.

My father while carrying rice sacks on his shoulders because of its heavy load while climbing mountains to transport it to nearest store he slipped, i received news from the neighbours that he fell down from the slope and his neck nerve got broken, He was immediately rushed to Patan hospital which was 179 kms from Khangsar due to non-availability of any nearby hospitals. By the time they reach hospital he died.

By the time i reached home to Khangsar after hearing news regarding my father's death my mother who was heart patient too lost her life due to cardiac arrest.

I and Aditya lost our Amma and Baba together on same day. It was shocking and tragic incident for both of us, but it was all god's wish, can't do anything except keeping them in prayers.

माँ-बाप का होना हमारे जीवन का आधार,

उनके बिना हर रोज़ लगता है अधूरा यह संसार

जब वे छूट जाते हैं, छूट जाता है सब कुछ,

माँ की गोदी, बाप के हाथों का स्पर्श

उनकी ममता की छाँव रहती है अनगिनत,

उनके बिना जीवन में होती है वहीनता

कौन समझाए दर्द यह, जो बिना कहे रह जाए,

माँ-बाप के बिना, कैसे जियें हम यह जिंदगी के राह में

उनके बिना हर पल लगता है बेजान,

उनके साथ ही था सब कुछ, उनके बिना अब कुछ नहीं

प्यार और स्नेह से भरी थी उनकी दुलार,

अब तो यादों में है वो, बिना उनके अब है संसार

जाते हैं वे एक दिन, होती है वह बिछड़ाई,

बस यादों में बसा रहती है उनकी मुस्कान फिर भी दिल की राह में

My uncle Harish Chandra was a nice and humble person and owns a Tempo Traveller. He told that he will teach me how to drive a mini bus so that i can carry passengers to and fro. In that way i can earn a living without depending upon anyone. But villagers are not going to leave me, they again started taunting me by saying : "सपना फर्किने बितिकै, यही तिम्रो स्थान हो।" ("ख्वाबों को उड़ने दो, तुम्हारी जगह यहीं है।"'', "उडान भर्नु पर्छ, तर यहाँको ध्यान राख।" ("उड़ान भरने से पहले यहाँ की संभलो!")

I didn't took their taunt seriously and decided to learn driving from my uncle and leave Khangsar forever with my brother but decided that i will comeback to pay respect to my parents once i become an officer.

Aditya completed his degree in B.Ed and returned back to Khangsar as college professor and taught the children in that way he paid respect to his mother.

Driving test day arrived and it was held at Suzuki Driving School, Lalitpur, Nepal. My luck was so bad that i failed in 1st and 2nd attempt of my driving test but i decided not to give up and in 3rd attempt i cleared my driving test with flying colours and received Light Motor Vehicle (LMV) license.

Later on with the help of my uncle Harish Chandra i decided to give further exams. I took training of heavy vehicle like bus driving and i gave the driving test and this time i cleared my driving test exam in 1st attempt itself and received Heavy Motor Vehicle (HMV) license. But my luck was nice and i received International Driving License by this i can drive vehicle in any country.

JOURNEY OF A BUS DRIVER

The journey of a bus driver is a unique blend of responsibility, skill, and daily interaction with diverse passengers and environments. It begins with rigorous training to obtain a commercial driver's license (CDL) and specialized training on specific bus models and routes'.

'Once on the job, bus drivers navigate through traffic, varying weather conditions, and different road types while ensuring passenger safety and adherence to schedules. They must manage stress and remain focused for long hours behind the wheel'.

'Interacting with passengers requires patience and good communication skills to provide assistance, information, and maintain a positive atmosphere on board. Dealing with unexpected situations like traffic accidents or passenger disputes requires quick thinking and decision-making abilities'.

'Despite challenges, bus drivers find fulfillment in providing a vital service to their community, ensuring people reach their destinations safely and on time. Each day brings new experiences and encounters, shaping their expertise and dedication to their profession'.

I later joined an travel agency in Kathmandu, Nepal which carries passengers from Kathmandu – Pokhara, Kathmandu – Delhi (International Route) etc... I took the charge of carrying passengers from Kathmandu – Delhi : 22 hr 2 min (1,190.5 km) via Agra - Lucknow Expressway to & fro. On the other hand i decided to continue my studies too & i decided to take up distance correspondence course in B.Sc (IT). I decided to study on my own expenses when the trip gets over at bus station in Delhi & Kathmandu respectively. At that time i was the first lady to ride on an international route. By looking at my hardwork, patience and dedication towards studies my colleague drivers supported me to learn and clear my exams alongwith paid salary so that my earning should not stop.

Few days later i went to Delhi to give my exams and luckily i again passed the exams in 1st attempt and that too by becoming a topper in university.

I decided to continue my job as tourist bus driver. This time i took Kathmandu – Mumbai : 35 hr (1,988.4 km) via Hindu Hrudaysamrat Balasaheb Thackeray Maharashtra Samruddhi Mahamarg.

This time my luck was about to take change. I was surprised to meet my school friend Alisha Rao with whom i used to study together since childhood and who was going to Mumbai as the prestigious Tata Mumbai Marathon (TMM) registrations were going on. She requested me to join her for 42.2 kms full marathon because she saw me running and practicing and also climbing the mountains with ease. Alisha took the responsibility of getting my TMM registrations done at any cost being an influencer.

JOURNEY OF A MARATHON RUNNER

The journey of a marathon runner is both physically and mentally demanding, often requiring months of dedicated training and preparation. It starts with setting goals, creating a training plan, and gradually building up endurance through long runs, speed work, and strength training. Nutrition and rest play crucial roles in recovery and performance'.

'During the marathon itself, runners face a test of their preparation, battling through physical fatigue and mental challenges such as self-doubt and pain. The support of fellow runners, spectators, and volunteers can be uplifting along the route'.

'Crossing the finish line represents the culmination of perseverance, determination, and hard work. It's a moment of immense satisfaction and accomplishment, regardless of finishing time. Post-race, recovery involves rest, hydration, and reflection on the experience, often followed by setting new goals or improving upon previous performances'.

'Overall, the journey of a marathon runner is a transformative experience that pushes physical limits, fosters mental resilience, and celebrates the joy of achieving personal milestones'.

My registration was accepted and allowed to participate in TMM full marathon. I got A gate while Alisha got C gate to assemble. New year started and January month arrived when the prestigious Tata Mumbai Marathon was going to take place from Victoria Terminus (VT) now Chhatrapati Shivaji Maharaj Terminus (CSMT).

No one can believe but i ran the TMM with ease as if i am doing it every year alongwith Kenya runners. Alisha completed her 42.2K in 04:00:00 while i completed my 42.2K in 02:00:00 with podium finish and with big amount of cheque.

Last i said thanks to Alisha for the golden opportunity. Alisha told me your hardwork and practice finally paid off. I will suggest you to participate in Comrades Marathon which happens in South Africa and which is scheduled in June but you need to practice daily to achieve target of 85.91 kms (12 hour run). The route is from Durban to Pietermaritzburg but don't leave your precious job. I said to Alisha 'what about the registration fees, passport & visa, accommodation i don't have enough money to pay for all?'. Alisha very politely and in friendly manner with smile said 'you don't worry about anything i will do all the formalities' you just concentrate on your job and practice'.

Alisha recited the poem which she learned during school days :

SATISH PUTHRAN
DREAMS TAKE FLIGHT : The Girl Who Dared

प्रातःकालको सजिलो प्रकाशमा, हामी जुता बाँधेर खडा छौं,

दुई साथी, एक-दूस्रा यस सम्झौताको प्रमाण गर्न तयार छौं

म्याराथन आगो लाग्छ, यो महान चुनौती हो,

तर हाम्रो साथ, साथै हामी यसलाई जित्न सक्छौं बिना कुनै समस्या को

घाटीहरू र पहाडहरूको बीचमा, संदेहले आउँछ जब,

म तिम्रो शक्ति बन्छु जब थकान गहिर्छ

हर कदममा, हाम्रो सम्बन्ध मजबूत हुनेछ,

हाम्रो आत्मा प्रेरित गर्दै, हामीलाई अगाडि बढाउँछ

सम्झना गर, हामी हाँसेर, र हाम्रो बीच जब रोइएको थियो,

बारे-बारे, तिम्रो साथ, तपाईं सधैं मेरो साथ छौं

अब चल, यो सपना पकड्नुहोस्, आज हामी यो प्राप्त गर्नुहोस्,

प्रत्येक मीलमा, साहस खोज्नुहोस्, रास्ता सजाउनुहोस्

संदेहले मुखमा, र पैरमा दुख्च, जब मेरो सम्झाउँछु,

साथी, तिम्रो रास्ता बनाउँछु, योजना बनाउँछु

प्रत्येक धडकनमा, प्रत्येक सासमा, हाम्रो साथ बढ्नेछ,

निराशाको पार गर्न साहस प्राप्त गर्नेछ

चल, दौड्नुहोस्, साथी, हृदय खोलेर बोल्नुहोस्,

यो म्याराथनमा, हामी सँगै हुनेछौं

प्रत्येक कदममा, सङ्गीतमा र छायामा,

SATISH PUTHRAN
DREAMS TAKE FLIGHT : The Girl Who Dared

हामी लेख्नेछौं यो कथा, जुन अनौठो हुनेछ र हाम्रो सबैको हुनेछ

किनकि अन्त चिन्ह, जहाँ विजयको चमक छ,

हरियो र आममा, हाम्रो सपनाको धुँध छ

यसकारण अगाडि बढ्नुहोस्, सूर्यको दिशा बढाउनुहोस्,

साथी, सँगै, रेस जित्न सम्म

✈ ✈ ✈

In the morning's early light, we lace our shoes,
Two friends, side by side, with everything to prove.
A marathon beckons, a challenge so grand,
But together, my friend, we'll conquer this land.

Through valleys and hills, where doubts may creep,
I'll be your strength when fatigue runs deep.
With each stride we take, a bond grows strong,
Fueling our spirit, propelling us along.
Remember the times we laughed and we cried,
Through thick and thin, you've been by my side.
Now let's chase this dream, let's seize this day,
In every mile, find strength to pave the way.

When doubts whisper low, and legs start to ache,
I'll remind you, friend, of the path we'll make.
For in each heartbeat, in each breath we share,
We'll find the courage to surpass despair.

DREAMS TAKE FLIGHT : The Girl Who Dared

So let's run, my friend, with hearts set free,
In this marathon, together we'll be.
With every step, in rhythm and rhyme,
We'll write a tale of endurance, one of a kind.

For the finish line waits, where victory gleams,
In the echo of cheers, in our shared dreams.
So let's chase the horizon, let's reach for the sun,
My friend, together, until the race is won.

I took my friend Alisha's words seriously and started practicing. Now the question arises to practice daily i should leave job or take transfer to Mumbai?. I has to select any one option. I approached my friend Maya Desai in Kathmandu regarding this matter. She helped me my job get shifted to Mumbai. It happened and now i can't quit my job and practice daily.

I was the girl who dared to give tuff competition to anyone without raising any question. All the formalities for Comrades Marathon completed, June month arrived and its time to fly to a new place outside India i.e South Africa. I was given warm welcome at airport by Kenya runners. I was so happy to see their kind gesture towards me.

Comrades Marathon (D-Day) arrived and race started. I was running continuously but while climbing hills i became little slow but completed the target of 85.91 kms in 06:00:00 and became 2nd podium finisher in my age category.

'NO DOUBT : NAKANJANI'

Now its time for me to concentrate on fulfilling my dream of becoming an Indian Air Force officer. I started to prepare for 'AFCAT (Air Force Common Admission Test)' in full swing which is scheduled in August.

I came across an advertisement in newspaper stating :

'AFCAT – Air Force Common Admission Test'

'Candidates are to apply as per the advertisement. The test is conducted all across India by the Indian Air Force'.

I departed to Bengaluru, Karnataka for my AFCAT online exam. I knew very well that AFCAT exam is not easy and so i tried to give my best in 1st attempt itself and reserved a seat myself for upcoming training.

29

CHAPTER IV

SATISH PUTHRAN
DREAMS TAKE FLIGHT : The Girl Who Dared

In the depths of chaos, a spirit bruised,
Where shadows loom and hope seems confused.
Through the labyrinth of doubt's fierce tide,
A heart beats strong, refusing to hide.

Fragments of light pierce the endless night,
Glimmers of courage, burning bright.
With each step, a battle fought and won,
A journey of healing, though just begun.

Through storms of fear and whispers cold,
Resilience blooms, a story retold.
In the echoes of pain, a voice resounds,
With strength unfurled, new purpose is found.

A tapestry woven with threads of grace,
From shattered pieces, a soul finds its place.
Embracing scars as badges of pride,
Rising from ashes, with wings open wide.

For in the heart's deepest, darkest parts,
Lies the power to mend and restart.
With each sunrise, a promise to reclaim,
A life rebuilt, beyond the fray's cruel game.

So, stand tall, oh warrior, fierce and bold,
Your spirit ablaze, a sight to behold.
Through disorder's grip, you've found the key,
To conquer, to thrive, to truly be free.

My training started and for few years everything was going perfect without any problem. But suddenly i fell down from a height when my training was going on. All my colleagues came running to see me exactly what happened to me. They tried to ask me what happened but i couldn't tell them because i was not knowing about it nor my Amma and Baba told me about my disorder.

They immediately rushed me to Command Hospital Air Force, Bengaluru for my treatment. Doctor took my brain MRI test and later informed my colleagues that there is a small brain tumor but not to worry, but this was not a good sign during my training period.

My senior officer in-charge of training advised me to take rest but i don't want at this crucial moment and i should give up so easily. On request of my fellow colleagues i finally decided to take a break of one week and advised me to take the medications on regular basis.

After a week, i resumed back my training journey with full confidence and strength and without any complications and problems.

I was 'Flying Cadet' undergoing training for 'Flying Officer'. There is a phrase which carries a deep meaning within itself *"If you have the will to do something, then nothing can stop you from achieving your goals"*.

Step by step i started clearing all my training alongwith exams without any fear.

For further training i was advised to report Air Force Academy (AFA), Dundigal which is premier training institution of the Indian Air Force. It is situated 43 kms from Hyderabad.

CHAPTER V

SATISH PUTHRAN
DREAMS TAKE FLIGHT : The Girl Who Dared

In the dawn's quiet breath, I stand,
Before the skies unfold their grand,
A heart that beats with purpose true,
To soar where eagles dare to pursue.

With wings of steel and spirit bold,
In the cockpit's embrace, I'll hold,
The dreams that lift me ever high,
Where freedom's wings unchained, shall fly.

Through clouds that veil the azure deep,
In silence where the heavens keep,
A symphony of stars that gleam,
My soul shall find its soaring dream.

For in this realm of boundless blue,
I pledge my courage, tried and true,
To serve with honor, strength, and grace,
In the Indian Air Force's embrace.

With every breath, with every flight,
I'll chase the day, I'll seize the night,
A cadence of duty, pure and clear,
Above the earth, in sky so near.

So here's my vow, before I soar,
To skies unknown and battlescore,
In wings of valor, I shall dance,
With pride, I take this daring chance.

SATISH PUTHRAN
DREAMS TAKE FLIGHT : The Girl Who Dared

For India's skies, I'll stand prepared,
With wings unfurled, I'll meet each dare,
To touch the heights where dreams take flight,
In the Indian Air Force, my heart alight.

Now the real test and journey will begin whether i really deserves to become an officer or just to sit home like other people in Khangsar and can't withstand against all the odds.

A significant journey of growth, responsibility and achievement within the military hierarchy.

In the quiet before the thunder roars,

I stand on the threshold of my fate,

Dreams aloft on wings of eagles soar,

As I prepare to enter the Air Force's gate.

With heart resolved and spirits high,

I lace my boots and don my blues,

Beneath the vast and endless sky,

I'll learn the art that few pursue.

Not just a cadet, but a soul in flight,

Bound to duty, honor, and the sky,

To chase the clouds in morning light,

SATISH PUTHRAN
DREAMS TAKE FLIGHT : The Girl Who Dared

And in the storm, not flinch or shy.

For here, amidst the roar of jets,
I find my purpose, clear and bold,
To serve with pride and no regrets,
In the Air Force's steadfast hold.

So here's to the journey, yet to unfold,
Before the cockpit and the pilot's seat,
With courage forged in steel and gold,
I'll soar high, my destiny complete.

I would like to share the basic ranks and stages of Indian Air Force which will help many aspirants like me who are dreaming to join the academy / force.

FLYING CADET TO WING COMMANDER RANKS

Flying Officer

|

Flight Lieutenant

|

Squadron Leader

|

Wing Commander

<u>Stages of Training for Flying Cadets in the Indian Air Force</u>

Initial Screening and Selection :

Pre-Selection Tests: Candidates undergo a series of tests including a written exam, pilot aptitude battery test, and medical examinations to assess their suitability for a flying career.

Interview: Selected candidates are then interviewed by a board to evaluate their potential and commitment.
Air Force Academy (AFA) Training :

Basic Training: Upon successful selection, cadets

begin their training at the Air Force Academy in Dundigal. This phase focuses on foundational military training, discipline, physical fitness, and basic aviation knowledge.

Ground Training: Cadets receive instruction in aerodynamics, aircraft systems, navigation, meteorology, and other essential subjects that form the basis of flying operations.

Flying Training :

Stage I - Basic Flying Training: Cadets start with basic flying training on single-engine aircraft like the Pilatus PC-7 Mk II. This includes learning the fundamentals of flight, basic maneuvers, and emergency procedures.

Stage II - Advanced Flying Training: Following successful completion of basic training, cadets transition to more advanced aircraft like the Kiran or Hawk. They learn complex flying maneuvers, formation flying, and combat training.

Operational Training :

Specialized Training: Cadets are assigned to specific aircraft types based on their performance and the Air Force's needs. This training includes advanced tactics, operational procedures, and mission-specific skills.

Commissioning :

Final Evaluation: After completing all training phases, cadets undergo a final evaluation to ensure they meet the standards required for operational duty.

Graduation and Commissioning: Successful cadets are commissioned as Flying Officers and are assigned to various operational units within the Indian Air Force.

Continual Professional Development :

Ongoing Training: Even after commissioning, officers continue to receive training and updates on new technologies, tactics, and procedures to ensure they remain proficient in their roles.

Stages of Training for a Flying Officer in the Indian Air Force

Selection and Induction :

Recruitment: Candidates go through a rigorous selection process, including written exams, pilot aptitude tests, and medical assessments.

Commissioning: Selected candidates are commissioned as Flying Officers upon successful completion of the initial selection process.

Initial Training at Air Force Academy (AFA) :

Basic Military Training: Newly commissioned Flying Officers undergo basic training at the Air Force Academy in Dundigal. This includes physical training, discipline, and foundational military skills.

Ground Training: They receive detailed instruction on aircraft systems, aerodynamics, navigation, and meteorology, which are crucial for understanding flight operations.

Flying Training :

Primary Flying Training: Flying Officers start with training on basic aircraft such as the Pilatus PC-7 Mk II. They learn fundamental flying skills, including basic maneuvers and emergency procedures.

Advanced Flying Training: After mastering the basics, they progress to more advanced aircraft like the Kiran or Hawk. This phase involves complex flying techniques, formation flying, and combat training.

Operational Training :

Type Conversion: Flying Officers are trained on specific aircraft types they will operate in their assigned roles. This includes detailed training on the aircraft's systems and operational procedures.

Mission Training: They undergo training tailored to specific mission profiles, such as air defence, transport, or reconnaissance, depending on their assigned squadron.

Integration into Operational Units :

Unit Posting: Upon completion of operational training, Flying Officers are posted to operational squadrons where they apply their training in real-world scenarios.

Continual Development: They engage in ongoing training and exercises to refine their skills and stay updated on new technologies and tactics.

Career Progression :

Advanced Courses: Flying Officers may attend advanced courses and participate in specialized training throughout their careers to assume higher responsibilities and leadership roles.

Leadership Training: As they progress, they receive additional training in leadership, management, and strategy to prepare for future roles in command and staff positions.

Stages of Training and Development for a Squadron Leader in the Indian Air Force

Initial Service and Experience :

Early Career: Squadron Leaders begin their careers as Flying Officers and progressively gain experience through operational duties, flight training, and participation in various missions and exercises.

Promotion to Flight Lieutenant: After demonstrating proficiency and dedication, they are promoted to Flight Lieutenant, allowing them to take on increased responsibilities.

Advanced Professional Training :

Command and Staff Courses: To prepare for the role of Squadron Leader, officers may attend advanced professional courses focused on command, leadership, and staff functions. These courses provide skills in managing personnel, planning operations, and strategic thinking.

Specialized Training: Depending on their role and aircraft type, officers may undergo specialized training related to their specific duties or new technologies in their field.

Leadership and Command Responsibilities :

Command Training: Officers selected for promotion to Squadron Leader undergo training designed to enhance their command skills. This includes learning advanced management techniques, leadership strategies, and operational command.

Operational Command: As Squadron Leaders, they are responsible for leading a squadron, managing resources, and ensuring effective performance during missions and daily operations.

Continual Professional Development :

Ongoing Training: Squadron Leaders participate in continual professional development to keep up with advancements in aviation technology, tactics, and leadership practices. This ensures they remain effective in their command roles and adapt to evolving challenges.

Career Progression: They are encouraged to engage in further education and specialized training to prepare for higher ranks and more complex responsibilities within the Air Force.

Evaluation and Assessment :

Performance Reviews: Regular evaluations assess their performance in command roles, leadership capabilities, and operational effectiveness. These reviews help in identifying areas for improvement and career development.

Leadership Roles and Future Opportunities :

Higher Command Roles: Successful Squadron Leaders may be considered for higher command positions, staff roles, or specialized assignments. They continue to build on their leadership experience and contribute to the strategic goals of the Indian Air Force.

Stages of Training and Development for a Wing Commander in the Indian Air Force

Early Career and Experience :

Progression from Squadron Leader: Wing Commanders start their journey as Squadron Leaders, gaining extensive operational experience and demonstrating leadership capabilities in their roles.

Promotion: With proven performance and leadership skills, officers are promoted to Wing Commander, taking on more significant responsibilities.

Advanced Leadership Training :

Command and Staff Courses: Wing Commanders attend advanced training courses designed to enhance their strategic leadership and management skills. These courses cover high-level command, staff planning, and strategic decision-making.

Specialized Training: They may also receive training tailored to specific roles, such as operational command, intelligence, or other specialized areas relevant to their assignments.

Operational and Strategic Roles :

Higher Command Responsibilities: As Wing Commanders, officers take on higher-level command roles, overseeing multiple squadrons or larger units. They manage complex operations, ensure strategic alignment, and lead significant missions.

Strategic Planning: They are involved in formulating and executing strategic plans, coordinating with other military branches, and contributing to the overall defence strategy.

Continual Professional Development :

Ongoing Education: Wing Commanders engage in ongoing professional development to stay updated with advancements in technology, tactics, and leadership. This includes participating in seminars, workshops, and advanced courses.

Career Growth: They are encouraged to pursue further education and training opportunities to prepare for senior leadership roles and more complex responsibilities.

Performance Evaluation :

Regular Assessments: Their performance is regularly evaluated through assessments and reviews. These evaluations focus on leadership effectiveness, operational success, and contributions to strategic goals.

Feedback and Improvement: Constructive feedback is provided to help Wing Commanders improve their skills and adapt to new challenges.

Future Opportunities :

Senior Command Positions: Successful Wing Commanders may be considered for higher command positions, such as Group Captain or Air Commodore. They continue to build on their leadership experience and contribute to the Air Force's strategic objectives.

Special Assignments: They may also be assigned to special roles or projects that leverage their expertise and leadership abilities.

The entrance exam undertaken by the Indian Air Force (IAF) for recruitment of officers is known as the Air Force Common Admission Test (AFCAT).

AFCAT is conducted twice a year by the Indian Air Force to select officers for various branches including Flying Branch, Ground Duty (Technical and Non-Technical) Branches. It consists of multiple-choice questions covering topics such as Verbal Ability, Numerical Ability, Reasoning, General Awareness, and Military Aptitude. Successful candidates proceed to further stages of selection including physical tests, interviews, and medical examinations'.

'AFCAT exam is conducted in cities such as Agartala, Ajmer, Ahmedabad, Aizawl, Alwar, Allahabad/Prayagraj, Ambala, Aurangabad, Bareilly, Behrampur (Odisha), Bathinda, Belagavi, Bengaluru, Bhagalpur, Bhilai, Bhopal, Bhubaneswar, Bhuj, Bikaner, Chandigarh, Chennai, Coimbatore, Warangal, Delhi and NCR, Dhanbad, Diu, ...'

'The AFCAT exam is held online (Computer-Based Test mode). There will be a total of 100 questions, which will be divided into four sections – General Awareness, Verbal Ability in English, Numerical Ability and Reasoning, and Military Aptitude Test'.

In the land where dreams take flight,
Amidst the skies of blue and white,

SATISH PUTHRAN
DREAMS TAKE FLIGHT : The Girl Who Dared

I trained with heart and steadfast might,
To serve my nation, strong and bright.

Now homeward bound, my heart elates,
To where my journey first began,
Where childhood dreams and future's fates,
Were woven into every plan.

Through trials faced and heights attained,
In wings of steel and courage trained,
I return, a transformed soul,
To the streets where memories roll.

Oh hometown dear, I come with pride,
A warrior of the azure sky,
Yet in your embrace, I find my guide,
To cherish moments, none can buy.

For dreams take flight, but roots run deep,
In every step and breath I keep,
In this place where my heart belongs,
Amidst the echoes of old songs.

So raise a toast to skies and earth,
To dreams fulfilled and new rebirth,
For I am home, yet still to soar,
With hometown love forevermore.

49

EPILOGUE

After many years, i returned back to my village as a beacon of hope of change.

I also set up scholarships under my name *'ANANYA SHARMA FOUNDATION'* for young girls, encouraging them to pursue their dreams fearlessly.

The once abandoned village of Khangsar begins to bloom with renewed aspirations, as more girls dare to dream of a future beyond tradition.

FINAL NOTE

SATISH PUTHRAN
DREAMS TAKE FLIGHT : The Girl Who Dared

In the hush of twilight's gleam, dreams take flight,
Where whispers of hope weave through the night.
They soar on wings of courage and might,
Painting the skies in hues pure and bright.

Through clouds that veil the vast expanse,
They dance, they rise, they take their chance.
Each dream a beacon, a cosmic trance,
A symphony of soulful resonance.

In the quiet depths where dreams reside,
They blossom, they thrive, they cannot hide.
In hearts that dare and minds open wide,
They journey on, a steadfast guide.

So let us cherish these dreams so bold,
Where stories untold are yet unfold.
In the tapestry of life they're sewn,
In every breath, they find their own.

For dreams take flight, beyond our sight,
They blaze a trail through darkest night.
With every beat of fervent might,
They shape our world in radiant light.

"DREAMS TAKE FLIGHT" is a testament to the power of resilience and the indomitable spirit of those who dare to dream.

My journey from a village shackled by customs to the limitless skies of the Indian Air Force is a reminder that no dream is too big and no obstacle too insurmountable for those with unwavering determination.

ख्वाब उड़ते हैं आसमान की ऊँचाइयों में,
हर इच्छा पांव धरा को छू जाती है वहाँ
जहाँ आकाश की कोई सीमा नहीं,
और दिल की हर मुराद पूरी होती है वहाँ

जगमगाते तारे सहारे रातें गुजारे,
हर चुनौती का सामना करना सिखाते हैं
क्योंकि ख्वाबों की उड़ान भी होती है मुश्किल,
पर उन्हीं में छुपी है सफलता की राह

ख्वाबों का रंगीन सफर, हर कदम एक नया मंज़िल,
जिद्दी रवानगी से बनता है सच्चा उड़ान का सफर
हार नहीं मानने वालों की यही कहानी है,
जो ख्वाबों को पंख लगाकर आसमानों में ले जाते हैं

POEMS BY AUTHOR

इसिका नाम है जिंदगी

एक वक़्त ऐसा भी आएगा,

एक वक़्त ऐसा भी मैं लाऊंगा,

एक वक़्त ऐसा भी आएगा,

एक वक़्त ऐसा भी मैं लाऊंगा,

जिन्होनें मुझे समझा नहीं और मुझसे नफ़रत करके अपनी दोस्ती तोड़ दी,

वो खुद एक दिन आएंगे,

वो खुद एक दिन आएंगे,

और मुझसे कहेंगे यार हमने तुझे समझने में बहुत देर कर दी,

तू जैसा भी था दिल का बहुत साफ और अच्छा था और जैसा भी था बहुत

सच्चा था,

मैं बस इतना ही कहूँगा,

मैं बस इतना ही कहूँगा,

अरे यारों बीती हुई बातों को भूल जाओ और गले मिल जाओ,

क्योंकि इसिका नाम है जिंदगी,

© ✍ सतीश

मंजिल जरूर मिलेगी

माना की चलने के लिए चुना हुआ रास्ता आसान नहीं,

माना की चलने के लिए चुना हुआ रास्ता आसान नहीं,

फिर भी चल देते हैं बस यही सोच कर और उम्मीद रख कर

एक दिन तो मंजिल जरूर मिलेगी,

मंजिल जरूर मिलेगी,

वो रास्ते ही क्या जिस पर कोई काँटे ना हो,

वो रास्ते ही क्या जिस पर कोई काँटे ना हो,

अजी जनाब, कांटों पर चलना अब आदत सी हो गई है,

ये ही सोच कर एक दिन मंजिल जरूर मिलेगी,

मंजिल जरूर मिलेगी,

चाहे कोई दोस्त अपना साथ दे या ना दे,

चाहे कोई दोस्त अपना साथ दे या ना दे,

ऊपर से कोई फ़रिश्ता ज़रूर आएगा और बोलेगा,

चल मेरा हाथ पकड़ तुझे तेरी मंजिल तक ले जाता हूँ,

अब हम बस यू ही चल देते हैं कि अगले मोड़ पर मंजिल जरूर मिलेगी,

मंजिल जरूर मिलेगी,

© ✍ सतीश

हारना मत

जीवन में लाखों खतरे आएंगे,

लाखो मुसिबत आएंगे,

लाखो रुकावते आयेंगे,

तू परेशान होकर गिरना मत,

रुकना मत,

क्योंकि तुझे हिम्मत नहीं हारनी है,

हारना मत

अपने हौसलों को बुलंद कर इतना,

अपने हौसलों को बुलंद कर इतना,

चाहे लाख तूफ़ान भी आ जाए,

तू परेशान होकर गिरना मत,

रुकना मत,

क्योंकि तुझे हिम्मत नहीं हारनी है,

हारना मत

जीवन में अपना साथ कोई दे या ना दे,

ये ऊपर वाला बैठा हुआ फ़रिश्ता तेरा साथ ज़रूर और हमेशा देगा,

क्योंकि तुझे हिम्मत नहीं हारनी है,

हारना मत

जीत हमेशा उसकी होती है,

जीत हमेशा उसकी होती है,

जो हारना नहीं जानता

क्योंकि वो जानता नहीं हारनी है,

हारना मत

तू खुद बन जा अपनी जिंदगी का सिपाही जो इतना शक्तिशाली हो,

जो आ ने वाला तूफ़ान उसका कुछ बिगड ना पाए,

क्योंकि तुझे हिम्मत नहीं हारनी है,

हारना मत

हारना मत

हारना मत

© ✍ सतीश

सपने

बुज़ुर्ग कहते हैं चादर उतनी ही फ़ैलाओ जितनी तुम्हारी औकात है,

बुज़ुर्ग कहते हैं चादर उतनी ही फ़ैलाओ जितनी तुम्हारी औकात है,

और सपने वो ही देखो जो आगे पूरा हो सके,

पर हमने नहीं माना,

पर हमने नहीं माना,

और सपने देखते रहे,

कब वो सपना टूट गया पता भी ना चला,

कब वो सपना टूट गया पता भी ना चला,

जब दिल को एहसास हुआ तब तक बहुत देर हो चुकी थी,

क्योंकि जेब भी एक बूटी कौड़ी नहीं हैं और हम सपने देखने चले,

बुज़ुर्ग ये भी कहते हैं,

बुज़ुर्ग ये भी कहते हैं,

सपने सिर्फ वो लोग ही देखते हैं जिनके जेब में पैसे हैं,

तुम्हारी तो कोई औकात नहीं बेटे,

तुम्हारी तो कोई औकात नहीं बेटे,

इसलिए सपने देखना छोड़ दो और ज़मीन पर आ जाओ,

जब तुम्हारे जेब में पैसे आ जाये तभी सपने देखना,

क्योंकि हर सपने हकीकत में नहीं बदल जाता है

© ✍ सतीश

ABOUT THE AUTHOR

SATISH PUTHRAN
DREAMS TAKE FLIGHT : The Girl Who Dared

Satish Puthran, born in Mangaluru, Karnataka on 08th October 1984 (Indian Air Force Day), was brought up in Bombay (Mumbai), Maharashtra. An animal lover and travel enthusiast by nature.

He is an alumnus of St. Mary's High School, Dahisar East, Mumbai : 1999-2000 batch. He has received the Best Student Of The Year award at St. Lawrence High School, Avdhoot Nagar, Dahisar East, Mumbai for the year 1991-1992.

He holds a Diploma in International Airlines, Travel, and Tourism Management with AMADEUS as the computer reservation system. He was a National Service Scheme (N.S.S) volunteer for 2 years under the University of Mumbai and completed the Civil Defence Academy (Basic & Warden Service Course) in Maharashtra. He is a professional marathon runner who can give tough competition to anyone.

He has participated in the Mumbai Ultra 12 Hour Run 2017 held on 13th August 2017, covering a distance of 55K without any prior practice. He has volunteered for many marathon events, including participation since 1st November 2015 (Karnataka Rajyotsava) at Central Park, Kharghar, Navi Mumbai for Mastek Foundation Run 2015 : 5K in 00:39:41.

He has participated in the Manipal Marathon 2019 in the 21K category, Manipal, Mangaluru, Karnataka (National Level) in February 2019, and broke his 21K timing at PKDM 2019 in March 2019.

He has volunteered with the Bhumi Mumbai NGO for many years and participated in various activities. He was involved in the Bhumi Nakshatra Sports event held at HP Nagar, Chembur, with Bosco Boys Home, Borivali West, Mumbai, Maharashtra, where he served as Shelter Home Manager for orphanage kids.

He was a Judge and Guest of Honour for Ghe Bharari presents 'Bal Mahotsav 2023 and Bal Mahotsav 2024, annual sports events for underprivileged kids held at Dr. M. G. Parulekar School, Vasai West.

Tour Guide with 'DK's Yatra Unlimited Holidays' for 'Mumbai (Dadar - Naigaon) - Trimbakeshwar - Shirdi - Shani Shingnapur' in March 2024 with '108' senior citizens onboard.

Currently co-author of two anthologies published by Thoughts Hymn Publishers, Noida, Uttar Pradesh, India. The anthologies are titled The Aurora's Embrace Volume 4 and Velvet Shadows Volume 1.

Received 1st Prize in Poetry Writing Competition held on Sunday, 18th August 2024 at Pejawara Mutt, Prabhat Colony, Santacruz East, Mumbai during 70th Annual General Body Meeting of Saphalya Seva Sangha, Mumbai.

REFERENCES

Comrades Marathon 2024
https://www.comrades.com/blog/posts/2024-comrades-marathon-route-distance-revealed

India Pakistan Air War of 1965
https://amzn.in/d/0bOCxjxY

The Mighty Eighth: A History of the Units, Men and Machines of the US 8th Air Force
https://amzn.in/d/00AZ4LM6

Wings Of Fire An Autobiography
https://amzn.in/d/09GRD2KQ

Wings of Fire: An Autobiography of Abdul Kalam (Hindi)/Agni Ki Udaan by A.P.J. Abdul Kalam: Soaring High in the Skies of Dreams and Determination - The ... of India's Missile Man (Hindi Edition)
https://amzn.in/d/0isFRK2I

AFCAT (Air Force Common Admission Test) Exam Guide
https://amzn.in/d/0f4XIl9B

Quantitative Aptitude for Competitive Examinations All Government and Entrance Exams (Banking, SSC, Railway, Police, Civil Service, etc.) 40 Videos | 2000+ Solved Examples | 10000+ Practice Questions
https://amzn.in/d/0egEUIY0

Objective General English -By S.P Bakshi- CDS, NDA, SSC, Banking, HM, MCA, B.Ed. Entrance And Other Examination
https://amzn.in/d/03TK1ARb

General Knowledge 2023
https://amzn.in/d/0gksIwEr

Let's Crack AFCAT - Air Force Common Admission Test - AFCAT Book
https://amzn.in/d/0bDURRKc

The Indian Air Force. Trends and Prospects - DTIC
https://apps.dtic.mil/sti/tr/pdf/ADA286789.pdf

13 Previous Year AFCAT Topic-wise Solved Papers (2011 - 2023) with 5 Practice Sets for Flying Technical & Ground Duty Branches 9th Edition | Previous Year Questions PYQs | Air Force Common Admission Test
https://dishapublication.com/products/13-previous-year-afcat-topic-wise-solved-papers-2011-2023-with-5-practice-sets-for-flying-technical-ground-duty-branches-9th-edition-previous-year-questions-pyqs-air-force-common-admission-test

Rank Structure – Indian Air Force
https://careerairforce.nic.in/indian-air-force-rank-structure

Tour of an abandoned village in the Nepal Himalayas
(Old Khangsar)
https://youtu.be/JUg9x8UB4eg?si=6pP_N0Fh7Wnq
URbk

FEEDBACK

FOLLOW ME ON

INSTAGRAM

SATISH PUTHRAN
https://www.instagram.com/08_satish_iaf
EMERGING AUTHOR
https://www.instagram.com/emerging_author_iaf

TELEGRAM
https://t.me/satish_08_iaf_iaa

TWITTER (X)
https://www.x.com/satishindianiaf

EMAIL
emerging_author_iaf@yahoo.com

DREAM BIG!!!